The Secret Adventures of Louie V

By Tracey Delio

Tracey Delio

To
Kate,
Enjoy!.

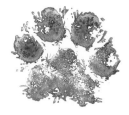

The Secret Adventures of Louie V

Written by Tracey Delio
Illustrated by Kit Grady

Manufactured in the United States of America.

For information, please contact:

The P3 Press
16200 North Dallas Parkway, Suite 170
Dallas, Texas 75248
www.thep3press.com
972-381-0009

A New Era in Publishing™

ISBN-13: 978-1-933651-36-1
ISBN-10: 1-933651-36-9

LCCN: 2008907730

Author contact information:
Tracey Delio

www.louievadventures.com

"Bye, Louie.
I'm off to work."

"MEEEEOOW," yelled Louie V.
She is finally gone! I fooled her into thinking I get lonely during the day.

1

Hmmm...
so much to do, and so little time.

Where do I start? In the bedroom, kitchen, or the bathroom?

Well, today I am feeling especially sassy, and the only thing to do with this fantastic feeling is to shop.

I have no pockets to
keep a wallet or money, so the only
place to go is HER closet! Yes, I will shop in HER closet!

It is true that I am a boy, but SHE must have something that would interest me.

The closet is always such a magical place! I am full of excitement! I don't know where to begin.

Shoes! Yes! I will start with shoes!

Bad idea. SHE only has two feet. Clearly I need four matching shoes...

"MEEEEEOOOOOOW" screamed Louie V. Watch out below!

Hmmm...how about shirts?

Scratch that! I don't have opposable thumbs to do the buttons.
That could get most frustrating!

Bags, pocketbooks—
that's the best idea! I need
a place to carry all my cat belongings.

13

Wait, hold the phone! How will I fashion this on my feline physique?

Hats! Yes, I love hats!

Baseball hats, sun hats, so many choices. What is a cat to do?
Too many decisions for my cat mind to handle!

Oh my! I must clean up before SHE comes home. It is not in my cat nature to leave my mess for someone else to tidy up.

Wow, all this shopping has made me quite sleepy.
Maybe if I just lay down...I can make an
educated decision...

18

"Oh, Louie V. Did you sleep the day away, you lonely boy?"

"Meeeeeooooooow," yelled Louie V.

Oh yeah,
that's what I did.

21

About the Author

Tracey Delio, M.A.CCC/SLP has been providing speech and language services to toddlers, preschoolers and school-age children on Long Island for the last 15 years. She holds a Master's Degree from Hofstra University and is also a Teacher of the Speech and Hearing Handicapped with a dual major in English. Past experiences include providing school- based therapy to Middle School and High School students with speech impairments and learning disabilities.

Tracey has worked extensively with other professionals on interdisciplinary teams which has broadened her knowledge base on a variety of disabilities. Her areas of special interest include motor speech disorders, sensory integration disorders, early language development and PDD/Autism Spectrum Disorders. She has worked side by side with ABA teams to facilitate speech and language development in the Autistic population. Tracey is a Certified PROMPT Instructor and teaches workshops in various locations throughout the United States.

Tracey is deeply involved in a number of charitable organizations including the Juvenile Diabetes Research Foundation, Autism Speaks and VH1 Save the Music. A portion of the proceeds from the sale of The Secret Adventures of Louie V will be donated to the aforementioned charities. Each of the charities support children and strive to make their future bright and prosperous. Information about these charities can be found on her website at www.louieadventures.com.

The author would like to acknowledge the following people:

My Family

Thank you so much for your love and support throughout this adventure.
Lisa, you helped my dream become a reality.
I am forever grateful.

Tracey